I0675587

ASSAD'S QUEEN

BY ROSA JAMES

Contact Information:

Email: misuselsnake@gmail.com

Website: Passion2Right.com

Cover Art by: Rosa James and Ariyon James

Published by Passion2Right 10/27 /2023

Edited By Chanekka Pullens

ISBN: 979-8-218-31292-3

1.   *Fiction*

Printed in the USA

Warning

This book contains fictional events that involve sex, violence, death, and inappropriate language.

This book is dedicated to anyone who is dealing with any type of trauma that has affected their life. Please know that you are not alone. If you are struggling talk about it and get professional help. I personally know that sometimes it's hard to take the first step to seek help but keep fighting because you have a purpose. Never feel like you are not worthy of love, support, protection, and happiness because you are.

TABLE OF CONTENTS

WARNING!!!

This book contains mild profanity, sexual content and
scenarios that could relate to true events.

CHAPTER ONE

I LOVE YOU

Chaya, we have been going strong for years and I am certain that I love you.

I was raised without my mother because she left me when I was five. My father was so heartbroken that he never allowed himself to fall in love with another woman. As I witnessed him take his aggression out on one woman after another, I found myself wondering if one of those women could have been the mother I needed.

The lack of a loving mother frustrated me, so I continued my father's toxic cycle. I became a master at womanizing and left a long trail of broken hearts. I truly felt I would never be a one-woman man.

Then my recklessness caught up with me when I was accused of rape. As I went through the process of trying to prove my innocence, I learned quickly that the world would turn their back on a black man.

One day in court, the judge asked me why I had sex with multiple women. That was the question that sent my life in a new direction.

After talking with my attorney, she suggested I go to therapy. My boys laughed at me, but I did not care because I wanted to change my toxic behaviors. I remember I met you the first week I started my therapy sessions.

Chaya, do you realize that you met me at one of the lowest points of my twenty-nine years on earth? Everyone on campus was looking at me as a rapist, especially the women. I remember you greeted me when I walked into the library. I looked into your eyes, and they were soft and carried no judgement.

Between court and therapy, I was struggling to keep up with my assignments. You let me stay in the library after hours to finish up my research paper.

Afterwards, we talked. While others asked me why I did it, you were the only one that asked me did I do it. The fact that you trusted me and gave me grace during that time in my life demonstrated that you were a true queen. You became my best friend and I had to make you my woman.

When we graduated from college, I was sure that I wanted to spend the rest of my life with you. And here we are well established in our careers. Baby, we have everything we want and need. We have the love and stability to take things to the next level.

Chaya, you are my soulmate, and I want my children to grow in your womb.

But there is one more piece that you have not given me. I see it when you drift away during conversations. The lack of eye contact you hold with men in general and you don't get angry, you rage. I need to know the entire you.

What wakes you up every night at 3:00am? Why do you hate yellow? Why do I only know the woman that I met in the library but not the things that made you who you are? If your past was painful tell me so I can help you like you helped me. I would do and go through anything with you, Chaya. I love you and want you to be my wife.

"Can you excuse me, Assad, I need to go to the bathroom," said Chaya, prying herself from his embrace.

He watched her naked body hurry to the bathroom before closing the door. When Assad heard the lock, he sighed before drinking the remaining wine from the bottle. He peeled himself from the plush rug and went into the kitchen to retrieve another bottle.

"Chaya, please trust me with your pain like you trusted me the day you met me!" yelled Assad while opening the wine. He exited the kitchen and sat the bottle next to the two empty wine glasses. He opened the curtains, displaying the beautiful view of the ocean. The sunset has been the best one he observed in the three days they spent at his father's beach home. "Baby, you are missing an epic sunset."

In the bathroom Chaya felt like a stranger as she looked into the mirror at herself. What she thought was another one of their getaways had a more important purpose. Assad was determined to tap into the woman he wanted to spend his life with. If things went his way, Chaya would be his wife and get pregnant. He confided in his therapist who suggested that whatever mystery she was keeping had to be so traumatic that she chose to suppress it. But we all know that unresolved emotions will allow you to bury them before slowly climbing their way back up to the surface. Most of the time this happens years later when you think you have completely moved on.

Assad refilled the wine glasses. He sat in the middle of the floor staring at the bathroom door. He had nothing but time on his hands and would be patient with his queen. He took a moment to pray that she would come out the bathroom and be transparent with him.

CHAPTER TWO

CHAYA

Just when you think that everything has turned out in your favor. Life has a way of bringing you right back where you started.

When I left my hometown of Kansas City, Missouri, I never wanted to look back. I went to therapy and trusted Jesus with my burdens. Then the door began to open, and I was able to follow my passion and live life. My confidence increased and my past stopped lingering in my mind daily.

Then I met Assad. I knew about the rape allegations but when I looked at him, I didn't see what everyone else was talking about. I felt comfortable with him and as time passed, I began letting my guards down slowly. I wanted him to focus on the beautiful, happy, productive woman before him. Not the girl that came from a broken foundation that was filled with trauma, lies, and drama.

How naive of me to think that he would never become curious about the life I left behind. I was content with him never finding anything out. I made his family mine and tried to forget about where I came from. I am afraid that sharing my past experiences and choices would make Assad look down on me.

This man is damn near perfect, and I am afraid of ruining things. He is patient and loves me correctly. He treats me like a queen. When he makes love to me, it's so magical. This man is the total package, so I must be good enough for him. I don't want him to know that I am broken. I don't want to be a liability.

We are the image of the perfect power couple. We both have demanding careers in the medical field. Assad is a heart surgeon, and I am an anesthesiologist, so we make great money. Now our love and success may be obsolete when I reveal my past.

My past is the reason why I had originally come to terms with the idea that I would be single for the rest of my life. But when I met Assad, I gave myself false hope. I knew a few women with a tarnished past. They were able to find husbands and lived happily ever after. I assumed I would be okay, but so much for that theory. The true lesson is that everyone's situation is different. Now my heart is pounding because I know tonight Assad is not letting this go.

Well, here we go.

An hour later, Chaya slipped into her robe, opened the door, and exited the bathroom. When she entered the room, the sight of her man standing on the balcony, shirtless, only wearing the grey gym shorts she loved was a turn on. It was scary how her sexual urge could arise in any type of situation. She was just in the bathroom crying, afraid to tell him her past. This was more validation that her past trauma still burned inside of her and dictated her life.

She joined Assad on the balcony. He welcomed her into his strong arms and kissed her on the forehead. His lips seemed to send an electrical wave through her body. She looked up into his eyes and puckered her full lips welcoming more gentle kisses. Assad guided her back inside to the rug and handed her a glass of wine. Chaya took a sip of the wine before getting comfortable between his legs. She rested her back on his broad chest and gazed out at the full moon hovering over the dark water.

They both shared silence for several minutes before Assad spoke. "This full moon represents you and the water represents where you came from. You were able to rise beyond where you came from, but the dark sky represents the darkness you still hold on to. But you are still able to shine no matter what."

Chaya admired how Assad was able to express things. As she continued to focus on the moon, she began to cry.

"Chaya, I love you no matter what, "Assad whispered.

Chaya sat up and drank the rest of her wine. She refilled her glass and sat Indian style facing Assad. "I just thought I could move and leave my past behind me. It was so dark and traumatizing. I worked so hard to forget but the fact that it's still difficult for me to discuss with you means that I have not healed. I know you say that you love me, but I am afraid that after I explain things, your perspective will change."

Assad sat up and positioned himself in front of her. He took the wine glass from her and put her hands into his. "Chaya, do you trust me?" She nodded her head. "Chaya, say that you trust me."

"I trust you, Assad."

"Then you know that you can tell me anything. Please tell me your deepest darkest secrets and I will prove that I still will love you, Chaya."

CHAPTER THREE

TRAUMA

From as early as I can remember, I have always felt my sexual drive. When in the room with a man and sometimes even a female, I could not help but to have a sexual thought. Why was I so young trying to hump little boys instead of playing normal games?

Years ago, my therapist asked was I molested as a child. Yes, I have one encounter that I remember during my childhood, but my sexual urges were present prior to that encounter. My therapist informed me that it was a possibility that something sexual transpired and I was just too young to aknowledge or remember it. It only takes one traumatic experience to make your life spiral out of control. I was sexually violated. The first encounter I remember was the one that changed me.

I was five years old when it happened. It was a Saturday morning in the eighties. When you did not have cable, you had to wake up early to catch the cartoons. I woke up, went downstairs, and turned on the television in the living room. I then went into the kitchen and fixed a bowl of cereal. The rule was not to eat in the living room, so I had my kitchen chair positioned to where I could get a clear view of the TV.

Usually while I enjoyed my cereal and cartoons everyone was asleep or at work. My mother worked two jobs and Saturday was her day to sleep in. My cousin Aktober was fast asleep in her bedroom; she usually woke up when her father or stepmother Renee came home from working overnight at their nightclub. This morning my uncle Elon was at home instead of at work.

While eating, he barged into the kitchen and started shouting at me. He said I was in trouble for being up so early in the morning. I responded that I always get up every morning to watch cartoons. He stood staring at me for several seconds before instructing me to go to the living room.

Now before I continue, I want to warn you to proceed with caution. This is my truth and just as hard as it would be for you to hear my story, it's harder for me to tell it.

When we made it to the living room, he took a seat in a chair and put me across his lap. When he started spanking me, I remember being so confused instead of crying. He kept stopping and readjusting me on his lap until I felt something warm against the front of my underwear. I was so confused. Then he stopped again and pulled my underwear down and started spanking me again.

At this point, I was sure that warm feeling was his penis. As he continued to spank me his breathing got heavier. Then he stopped and allowed me to stand up. I stood there in shock at my confirmation. The sight of Uncle Elon's brown penis would be embedded in my mind forever.

He grabbed my arm and started pulling me towards him again. I used my weight to help me pull back from him, but his grip was tight. I kept pulling back while saying no. He tried to bargain with me. He said he would buy me ice cream and give me money. When I began to cry, he released his grip causing me to fall on my butt. While I hurried to pull up my yellow underwear, he demanded me to go back to the kitchen to finish my cereal.

But I was not hungry anymore; I just wanted to go upstairs and hide. As I passed those stairs leading upstairs, I wanted to dash up them.

At this moment this man was so scary to me. I was afraid to yell for my mother because I thought he would hurt her. Aktober was the same age as I. I hoped she would not come down because he would probably try and do the same thing to her.

I sat in the chair and tried to resume eating my cereal, trying to ignore the dead roach floating around in it. Uncle Elon stood in the doorway staring at me.

I just kept my head down hoping he would just go away. Was he standing there thinking of what else he could do to me? I was afraid and confused. Why was this happening to me?

Suddenly, he became impatient and revealed a belt. He approached the table and began spanking me, not caring about where the belt landed. The belt buckle left a scar on my wrist that is a daily reminder of that morning.

He continued to beat me while speaking the words, "You bet not tell anyone."

He did not stop until I verbally agreed.

Then he ordered me to go upstairs. I scurried around him and ran upstairs, passing my mother's bedroom. I went to my Aunt Lane's bedroom on the top level of the house. She never seemed to be home but when she was, I spent all my time with her. I missed her when she was away.

I sat on a milk crate and stared out the window trying to process what just happened. Several minutes passed before I heard Uncle Elon's heavy body walking up the stairs. Every creek made my stomach turn in knots. He stood in the doorway and demanded me to get into the bed. I obeyed and hurried to the bed and hid under the covers. Then there was dead silence. My heart pounded as I prayed that he would not come over to the bed. I was relieved when I heard him going back down the stairs. When I heard the front door close, I hurried out of the bed and went to the window just in time to witness him going out the gate and walking up the street.

I went back to bed, laid down, and wept until I fell asleep. I slept so long, Aktober and my mother came to check on me. I lied and said I was not feeling well. I stayed in my aunt's bedroom all day just watching television.

Moving forward, whenever I woke up on Saturday mornings, I would creep down the stairs and peek around the corner to see who was downstairs. If it was not Aktober, my mother, Aunt Lane, or Grandmother, I would stay upstairs until the coast was clear. Even til this day, yellow triggers the memory of what happened.

As for Uncle Elon, he carried on as if he had done nothing to me. Months later, I confided in my Aunt Lane about what happened. After listening, she went to my grandparents and told them. During the conversation, I remember sitting in my Aunt Lane's room nervous about whether I was going to get in trouble. Then she came to get me and took me to my grandparents. She told me to explain what happened. I told them the same thing I told her. Afterwards, there was a long period of silence before they dismissed me without any words of comfort.

Later when Uncle Elon came home, I remember my grandparents talking to him on the front porch for a very long time. Then later that night, I was awakened by the sound of arguing. My mother came to me and asked me what happened, and I explained it again. She left the room and never brought it up again. For the next few days, I did not see Uncle Elon around.

I was sure that my grandparents put him out on his ass for violating me. But a month later he returned. My Aunt Lane was so angry, she left and that was the last time I saw her alive. My grandmother's brother, Uncle Clifton, and Aunt Renee saved up enough money to buy a home. They allowed my mother and I to live with them. My older brothers Marshall, Hunter, and Jewl were still living with our father. They had no idea what was going on but would come over to visit from time to time.

Back then instead of addressing issues most families swept things under the rug. You were forced to forget about your trauma and move on. All the while, the person that violated you walked around like nothing ever happened.

Whenever we went to visit our grandparents, I had to face Uncle Elon. But what made it worse was that everyone was cool with him. It sickened me to watch my mother joke with her little brother like he had never done anything to her daughter. It was like she chose him over me,

and I hated her for that.

CHAPTER FOUR

NO HEALING ALLOWED

What Uncle Elon did to me changed me.
I thought about sexual acts all the time especially
when I was around boys or older men. If a boy
showed any interest in me, I assumed our
communication had to be sexual. But on the flip
side, I was terrified when around men that I did not
want to be sexual with. The only men I could be
around and be comfortable was my brothers,
father, and Uncle Clifton.

When my mother and father got back
together, we moved into our own place. Things
were going great the first year but then my parents
began fighting all the time. It got so bad that my
father had to move out; this time he left my
brothers. He would come by and visit us every
week. Eventually, it turned into barely once a

month. My mother had to pick up a second job again, so I hardly saw her. Things were hard without my father around. Money was low all the time and my mother did not qualify for public assistance.

That's when my brothers started hanging out in the streets hustling and robbing people. No one was paying attention to me, so I was able to do as I pleased and just had to figure out things myself. That was not good because not only was I too young, but the effects of my trauma had me displaying some unhealthy behaviors.

Being promiscuous was my language. I wanted to be an adult and find a man so we could be together. Since I was not getting love and attention at home, I would seek it elsewhere. I just wanted to be accepted. If letting the boys do what they wanted with me would get that attention then I was okay with it.

Then things changed when a boy showed interest in me at school one day. Instead of asking him to the movies, skating, or day out at the mall, my fast ass asked him if he wanted to meet in the janitors closet to fuck. I remember giving him the letter after school. I knew he would meet me there, so I spent the evening before preparing myself. When I dressed for school the next morning, I wore a skirt for easy access and a pair of thong panties my friend Harper stole for me from the mall.

I stepped off the bus and walked into the school with confidence. It sounds so silly now, but it made sense to me then. When I went into my first hour of class his desk was empty. Maybe he was running late for school or maybe he was in the janitor's closet waiting for me. I lied to the teacher and told her I felt sick. She gave me a pass to the nurse's office, and I went to the janitor's closet instead. I hurried inside so no one would see me.

He was not there, so I waited a few minutes figuring we were missing each other. As I waited someone came into the closet. It was not Mr. Pearl the janitor because he was out sick.

This man wore a janitor's uniform and was much younger than Mr. Pearl who was at least in his sixties. He questioned why I was in the closet while taking a seat at the edge of the desk. I tried to think of a quick lie, but nothing came out. He smiled and told me don't worry he would not tell. I sighed in relief. Then he asked me again why I was in the closet. I told him the truth. After listening to me patiently he told me that my problem was that I was looking for a little boy and not a man. He locked the door, and everything happened so fast. Next thing I knew, I was lying on the floor enduring the pain of him entering me. I did not make a sound. When he finished, he got up and went over to the sink to clean himself off.

He turned around and tossed me a rag and instructed me to clean myself up before he exited the closet. I stood at the sink cleaning myself. As I rinsed the bloody towel off in the sink, I didn't know how I was supposed to feel. I never told him no, so was I raped? How would I explain why I was even in the janitor's closet? I hurried out the closet and went to my gym locker and retrieved a pair of underwear to slip into. The bell rang just in time for me to get to my second hour class. For the remainder of the morning, I sat quietly in a daze thinking about what happened.

After lunch, the counselor called me into her office about the letter I had given to the boy. He turned the letter over to his parents and they notified the school. Now I was beyond embarrassed, and I ached from what just happened in the closet. I knew that I could not talk about it because who would believe me. My own mother didn't care that my uncle tried to rape me so why would this stranger care what happened? Especially when I was trying to have sex with another student.

The counselor asked me if anyone had ever touched me. She assured me that she would not violate my confidentiality. This was the moment that someone could help me get over the trauma I experienced and help me deal with my promiscuous feelings. I told her about Uncle Elon.

When I was finished explaining she gave me a hug. I felt uncomfortable because I never received hugs. For me, kisses, hugs, certain voice tones, and long stares meant there was going to be sexual contact. When I watched people show affection, I always assumed that something fishy was going on.

She released her embrace and looked at me in my eyes before telling me that she had to speak with my mother to make sure things were safe in the home or else she was required by law to contact child protective services.

During that time, I was in the sixth grade and my brothers were in high school. We had too much going on in our household for CPS to get involved. All my mother did was work and sleep, my father never checked on us, and my brothers were running amuck breaking the law and running random females in and out the house.

That afternoon when I rode the school bus home, I sat at the front of the bus instead of the back. I had to figure out how to tell my mother that she had to come to the school and talk with the counselor.

When I made it home, my brother Jewl was on the front stairs talking to one of his new girls. He must have seen the worry in my face because as soon as I entered the front door he was on my heels. Jewl was fifteen, the youngest of my three brothers.

During this time, he was formulating a reputation for the streets so he was always looking for the drama so he could enforce it. Hunter was sixteen. He dropped out of school with plans to pursue his GED but instead he got wrapped up in the street life of robbing and hustling. Marshall had just turned eighteen and he already had a reputation and a little money in his pocket. It was his final year in high school, and he planned to go to college. He was the man of the house. He controlled the environment and kept us in check for the most part.

Jewl caught me before I went up the stairs to my bedroom. "Hey, sis, what's wrong? Some niggas fucking with you? Just point them out," were his exact words.

My emotions had been so discombobulated all day and the way he cared when he spoke provoked my tears. He hurried to me and guided me to the couch. When we both sat down, he was already riled up anticipating who he would be after. He knew that if his sister was crying then that meant it was serious because I never cried since the day Uncle Elon violated me.

I opened my mouth and told him everything from Uncle Elon, the note I wrote, and what happened in the Janitor's closet. When finished, his light skin was damn near pink all over. He took my hand, and we left the house to go find Hunter and Marshall. They were not far because they had a small house a block away where they only hustled and gambled. The place was a ticking time bomb because they were basically squatting until the owner, or the police made their presence. For them, squatting kept them off the corners where most hustlers died or were arrested. Jewl approached Marshall and told him we all needed to talk.

We went to grab something to eat and went over to this lowkey park on the west side of town. Marshall was hood but he loved his peaceful places. His goal was to get us out of the ghetto and move us into a nice quiet neighborhood. Marshall had three personalities. He was our dad, a street nigga, and the corny guy. On this day he was the corny guy, being polite to the old ladies at the park, picking up trash in the walkway, and engaging in small talk with people we had never seen before.

Hunter could not stand it when Marshall acted like that because he lived by the street code. He was a humble beast, solo, calculating, never barking; he just went in for the kill. When Hunter talked, you listened because he rarely talked. When you thought he was not listening he was hearing it all. The OG's loved Hunter because of the way he carried himself. He was particular about who he dealt with, he didn't really fuck with a flock of women like Marshall and Jewl. He had been in and out of juvenile since age twelve all for violent crimes.

We took a seat and ate until Marshall finished his conversation with a black woman that was dressed like a teacher. When he came over to join us, Hunter looked up from his food and mocked him. He always called him a company man when he irritated him. Marshall would always display his charming smile and tell Hunter, "You should have stayed in school."

We took time to laugh at Marshall's and Hunter's bickering before getting to the serious discussion. Jewl told me to tell them everything I told him. As I explained everything like before, my brothers stared at me. I could not tell how they were taking the information, but I felt a weight lift off me with every word.

When finished, I began to cry in relief. They let me cry for a few minutes. When I finally finished, Marshall took my hands into his and squeezed them, Jewl put his arms around me.

Hunter reached across the table and wiped my tears away before saying, "Today is the last day you cry, sis."

From that point moving forward, my brothers raised me to SURVIVE and ENDURE not to heal. I got my brother's attention but there was still another obstacle.

The next day at school, I sat in my class nervously because I still had not told my mother what happened. I figured my brothers had an escape plan to get away from child protection services because they told me not to tell her.

In my mother's eyes she had the perfect children. When she came home from work things were always in order. She had no idea that Hunter dropped out of school because he had a woman that made fake report cards for him. Jewl only went to school for drama. Marshall and I got good grades, so we didn't have to lie. In fact, getting good grades was all I had going for myself. I figured it would be my way out of the life I was living.

So, as I sat at my desk not sure where I would be by the end of the day, the counselor called me to the office. I gathered my things, exited the classroom, and walked down the hallway. I pondered whether I should just run out of the building. But when I saw Jewl in the hallway sitting on a bench outside the office, he gave me a thumbs up and said that everything was okay. I went into the counselor office where Marshall and the lady from the park that I said looked like a schoolteacher sat.

The woman came up to me and began hugging and kissing me, then she whispered in my ear to play along. She guided me to one of the chairs before sitting next to me. "Honey, I had no idea this happened to you. My God I wish I would have moved away from my parent's house sooner. My right hand to God you will never have to worry about anyone else ever violating you. If only you would have told me, your Uncle Elon would never have made it long enough to have a stroke and die."

The woman was so good, I felt like she was really my mother apologizing. It felt good to hear her words. We all exited the office, and the woman signed me out early. The counselor was satisfied and never bothered me again.

I guess you are wondering why not just tell my mother. At this point, my brother's idea worked and there was no need. I know this was the wrong way to handle it. My mother needed to know; I needed therapy. But my brothers were young black boys raising themselves and a little girl. They knew that at their age they would not find a wonderful foster home so what was the point. Their perception was to make me strong so that I could survive. They did not know how to help me heal from my trauma because they battled with their own every day. They had no positive role models to show them the right way. Experiencing poverty, they wanted money and success, they wanted to be acknowledged and accepted by their peers, they did not want to walk around a product of a struggling mother.

Unfortunately, they unknowingly were feeding my trauma by the environment they created around me. I watched them run women in and out and treat them badly. They did not realize that the type of relationships they demonstrated to me would be the ones I would endure.

It was an environment of trauma bonding. The women they hung around all came from toxic situations. They were violated just like me, broken, and had no goals for themselves. They just wanted attention and protection from the man they wanted which in their eyes was the definition of love.

I was the little sister, so they had to stay in my good graces when they hung around. Most of them were able to connect with me because I could relate to their traumas. But when I think about it now, these young ladies were just ass fucked up as I was. Their perception of things was so distorted. And just like me they had a high level of sexual behavior. I witnessed women fighting over my brothers, spending all their money on them, boosting for them, even committing crimes. The ones they trusted stayed around the house keeping it clean, cooking, and spending time with me. In fact, when I got my period, it was one of Hunter's girls that taught me all I needed to know.

Over time some of these girls became a form of family to me and I listened to them. I had two friends, Grace and Harper. They both came from toxic homes also, so they practically stayed at my house. The low esteem toxic women were our mentors. The only difference between me and my friends was that I had my brothers pulling my coattail from time to time. They reminded me that if I was going to be a hoe then I was going to be a smart and dangerous one.

CHAPTER FIVE

LICENTIOUS

I put on the bright red cheap lipstick that I purchased from the hair store and exited the bathroom. I was being careful not to get caught by Hunter who was chilling on the couch watching television. I lowered my head and walked past him before hurrying out the front door. Once I made it outside, I dashed across the street and disappeared into the apartment complex. I looked back often to make sure no one had spotted me.

When I was halfway to my destination, I felt relieved. I knocked on the front door softly and looked over at his bedroom window. The light came on and a few seconds later the front door opened.

Nelson hurried me inside and to his bedroom. His parents were home, but they were always upstairs in the bedroom chilling, not realizing that their 16-year-old was sneaking a girl into the house almost every day except for the weekends. But when I think about it now, they probably did not care because there was a picture of Nelson and his girlfriend Tina on one of the end tables in the living room.

You know how some couples looked like they belonged together physically? That was Nelson and Tina. So much so that they almost looked like siblings. He told me about her the first time we met at the park down the street several months ago. Maybe I should have questioned why he was pursuing me if he had someone. But I did not because this was my chance to get attention from someone. I always wanted a boyfriend or someone close to one and Nelson made me feel like I had someone.

I can't say that I was even jealous of Tina; she visited every Friday and Saturday. I was not allowed to come on those days. It was crazy how it did not bother me then as much as it bothers me now. But that just shows that I had developed self-worth that I did not have during that time.

Nelson and I had conversations, but they didn't have much value, or I was not listening. I was on a tight schedule, and I didn't understand at that time that spending time with a boy did not have to consist of sex. I didn't know what to talk about with him anyway. The sex was giving me a temporary connection to him that I needed. When it was over it was like it never even happened.

What did I want out of this situation? I had no standards set for him, I had no goals, I kept myself restricted to that bedroom laying on my back.

Then one day it all ended, and it was not my decision. Tina picked up a couple extra days during the week to spend at his house. I remember coming over one day and Nelson hurried outside to meet me. That day we sat on his porch and had the longest conversation we ever had during the seven months we were fucking. The conversation ended with him breaking things off with me. He said I was boring and all I wanted to do was have sex. He asked me what type of music, movies, and food I liked; I could not answer him. He laughed in my face and told me he would see me around before leaving me on the porch by myself.

When I made it home and came in the front door on that day, Hunter noticed the lipstick for the first time and gave me a lecture. He told me that the lipstick made me look like a whore and that men would not respect me. I sat quietly listening to his words. I was thinking how it would have been more helpful to hear seven months ago. He made me bring him the lipstick and he trashed it before sending me back upstairs to my room.

It took me years to understand what Nelson was talking about. He was telling me that I did not know myself. I was not interesting, I had no substance, so I was only attractive until the man got the panties. Tina had enough to keep him around and I envied her for that. Based on the photo she was pretty. I imagined her being confident. She probably had standards so high that she could keep Nelson challenged. She had what it took to not have to go directly to the bedroom.

How could a girl be so intriguing to me but a stranger? Was it because she was able to keep something I lost? Hell, I wasn't even sure if I really wanted Nelson at that time because I was just focused on sex. After Nelson dumped me, I stuck close to home, around moping with absolutely nothing to do or look forward to. Hunter's girlfriend Scarlett noticed I was down and tried to cheer me up. I liked talking to her because she was different. We talked about things outside the box like Shakespeare, other countries, artists, and classical music.

Scarlett was about living a free life where you could express yourself. She taught me how to meditate and we made plans to travel to Egypt when I turned eighteen. She said Hunter would have enough money by then to pay for the both of us.

Luna could not stand Scarlett and the relationship we had. I think she just could not relate to Scarlett, so she was intimidated by her presence. Luna hated the fact that Hunter was with her. She felt that Hunter was a sellout for having a relationship with a white girl. You see, in my house being with a white girl was not ideal. My mother had her reservations about it but never voiced them as strongly as Luna did. Her reasons were that my father cheated on her with a white woman, and she never healed from that. Hunter advised me to never look at color first and always get to know a person for who they are instead of putting everyone in the same basket.

Now that I think back there were some positive influences going on, but the negative seemed to bury them. It takes more energy to forget about something bad than to focus on the good and keep pushing. In fact, it seemed like every time I got comfortable, and things were looking good something happened that would add to my list of traumas.

Weeks later, I was sound asleep in bed when Marshall woke me up at 3:00am. He instructed me to get dressed in dark colors. I didn't think anything of it because Marshall never involved me in dangerous stuff like Jewel. Thanks to Jewl, I was in roaring gun battles, saw him beat the hell out of people, and even participated in a few drive bys.

We exited the house and got into a car. As I rode, I kept thinking how raggedy the car was and it was clearly not Marshall's taste. We arrived at a wooded area. Marshall parked, turned off the engine, and instructed me to get out the car. We walked to the trunk and when he opened it, the janitor that raped me was hogged tied with his mouth covered with duct tape. I never told anyone this because I did not want to risk anyone snitching on my brother.

Marshall picked up the gasoline can and poured some on the man's face waking him up. When the man saw me, his eyes bulged but he closed them fast because gasoline got in his eyes. I am sure he recognized me because he began trying to talk.

"This the man that raped you, right?" questioned Marshall.

I nodded. He took his gun out and shot the man twice before setting him on fire. We watched the car burn for a few minutes before walking several blocks to a gas station where he called Jewl to pick us up. While we waited for Jewl, we talked. Marshall told me that it took a while for him to find the man, but he had to. He wanted to show me what retribution looked like since I had not received any for what Uncle Elon did. That night, he gave me the apology that I needed from my mother. He said that he would do whatever he could to protect me moving forward.

My brother was trying to fill some of the voids I had endured from my trauma. This made me feel bad because my trauma was affecting everyone. The guilt made me think about Harper who would never receive retribution for her trauma because she didn't have brothers like me. She was ganged raped at a party and contracted herpes. The group of men lied and said she allowed them to run a train on her. Poor Harper was so embarrassed she didn't have the courage to press charges. She just wanted it to go away.

Grace was in foster care and had to constantly fight her foster mother's nephews and sons who always tried to have sex with her. Her foster mother knew it was happening and said that no orphan was going to get her family in trouble. So, Grace ran away from home. Her foster mom didn't bother to report her missing because she was still receiving the checks. Grace spent a lot of time at my house with me. However, when my mother lost her job, she was around more and was cracking down on the company.

Sometimes Jewl would let her sleep at the spot in exchange for her cleaning it up. But once Luna got wind of that, she was convinced they were fucking and shut that down. She beat the hell out of

Grace, causing her to run off in the middle of the night. I didn't see her for months.

One day, I was coming out the library downtown and there she was homeless and strung out on drugs. When I approached her, she was so high she did not recognize me. Marshall pulled up and told me that I had to let her go and she would come back when she was ready. I resented my mother for not helping Grace and hated Luna for running my friend away.

My friends' traumas were far worse than mines and I carried the guilt of that. I tried to bury mines because their issues were really the ones that called for a burning body in the trunk of a car. I was being all complicated about my uncle trying to molest me. I was only raped in a closet because I was waiting for another person to come have sex with me and I brought that on myself. But Grace and Harper were being continuously raped and had to take extreme measures to cope with their trauma. It altered their lives, and I was able to at least leave mines behind. That guilt made me feel unworthy for years until I realized that trauma was trauma no matter how small it seemed to be.

CHAPTER SIX

PREDITORS

Harper finally convinced me to try older men again. I snuck out of the house one night and attended a college party with her. We were having the time of our lives. College kids know how to have fun, the drinks were plentiful, and the guys were fine.

That's when I met Andrew. He said he was from California and was attending college to become a teacher. He was also an assistant coach for high school basketball. I learned soon that the high school was his hunting grounds. He was cute so the girls went crazy over him, and he had the nice car to attract their attention.

That night at the college party he was very accommodating. He made sure we had drinks and kept us entertained. When the party was over, instead of letting us get into a cab, he drove us to my house. He gave me his number and told me to call him if we ever wanted to get out again and have fun. I fell for the fact that he didn't try anything with me that night. I figured it was a sign he was a good dude.

I waited a few days before calling him because I did not want to seem desperate. For the next few weeks, we had great conversations on the phone. When we finally went on a date, he took me to a movie, and we went out to eat afterwards. I was outdone when he dropped me off at home again without any sex.

His moves really had me in my thoughts. That night I laid in bed thinking about how Nelson said I didn't have any substance. Andrew would be my chance to learn how to connect with a man on a level other than sex. I set goals to be more involved in conversations because Andrew was a talker.

Since he was into sports, I started watching sports and that became our thing. He would invite me to some of the high school games and afterwards we would go grab a bite to eat and talk about the game. He even met me at the library a few times to help me with some of my work assignments. He was smooth, dressed well and kept his hair cut low with a neat line. I had a major crush on him but after time passed, he just seemed like a big brother from another mother.

He had a one-year-old son and from time to time we would pick him up and take him to the park. I really liked who Andrew was. He was smart, stable, responsible, generous, and funny. I was enjoying the attention he was giving me. Then as we all know what lies in the dark comes to light. While waiting in the car one day, I came across his driver's license. This man was 30 years old! I never asked him his age, I assumed he was in his early twenties because he looked it.

I wanted older but not by that much because I was only 14 years old. At this point, I should have asked him why he wanted a girl who was barely in high school. Now I wondered how old his baby mother was. I didn't speak up and continued dealing with him despite the red flags. One night, he called me and told me to skip school the next day and he would pick me up. Andrew never allowed me to skip school when I suggested it before. He picked me up early Wednesday morning and we drove for at least a half hour ending up in Kansas.

He parked in front of a small house, and we exited the car. I noticed a mustang parked in the driveway. I followed him to the front door. He used a key to enter while informing me this was where he lived. When I entered, there was a man sitting on the couch playing the video game. Andrew introduced me to Sabastian and informed me that he was his roommate. It felt good knowing that he was not shacked up with a woman. He went into the kitchen and came out with a couple of wine coolers. We sat on the couch and watched Sabastian play the game for about an hour before retreating to his bedroom.

When I entered the bedroom, I was disappointed. This room did not reflect the person I saw. His bed was a twin mattress on the floor. His nineteen-inch television sat on a milk crate, and there was a pile of clothes on the floor in the corner of the room. The walls were bare and there were sheets in place of curtains. The closet was open and there were no clothes inside or shoes. So where was he storying all this gear he was wearing? I was convinced this had to be a trap house.

I was feeling a little buzzed, so I took a seat on the mattress. He turned on the television and sat beside me and asked me if I was okay. When I said yes, he suggested that I take my shoes off and relax more. I did just that. We laid in his bed watching television for a few minutes before he began grinding on me. I remember feeling sensations between my legs because his grinding felt good. I never felt like this with Nelson, so this was a good thing I thought.

He began kissing my neck while easing his hands under my shirt. I kept feeling the throbbing sensation between my legs as he continued kissing and rubbing on me. When I was relaxed, he climbed on top of me and begin pulling my pants down. I laid there and let him have all the control. He stood to his feet and took off his clothes displaying his erection. I watched him put a condom on before he climbed back on top of me. He eased inside of me. I closed my eyes and welcomed him because it felt good.

I remember thinking how it was well worth the wait. Then the bedroom door opened, and Sabastian entered naked. My heart began to pound, and Andrew felt it because he told me to calm down and go with the flow. Sabastian got on the mattress with us, and he began sucking one of my breasts while Andrew continued to pump away. I let it happen.

Then the unthinkable happened, something I was not ready to handle at my age. Sabastian and Andrew started kissing each other. My body went numb as I watched them make out with each other. Then Sabastian got on top of me and began pumping away as Andrew was on his knees with his dick in my face jacking off. Then they both stopped focusing on me and finished pleasing each other. I laid there frozen, not sure if I should leave the room or not. I had never seen two men together. It was the early nineties and being homosexual was not open as it is today.

When they were finished Sabastian left the bedroom and Andrew laid beside me. He asked me was I okay, and I nodded. We showered and got dressed before leaving the house. I remember walking past Sabastian; he just focused on the video game, as if nothing ever happened. The ride home was quiet, and I could not wait to get out of the car. When we made it to the gas station, I hopped out of the car without saying goodbye. I don't recall Andrew saying anything either.

That experience humbled me for a moment. I was afraid to deal with anyone older than me. I stopped going to the school games to avoid seeing Andrew.

One day, I was walking home from the bus stop and Andrew pulled up. He instructed me to get inside the car. I wanted to run but for some reason my stupid ass got inside the car. Why was I like this? We drove around the corner to an apartment building. After parking in the back of the building, he didn't waste any time invading my space and kissing me.

Once again, I went numb. We only made it to second base before someone drove into the parking lot. Paranoid, he stopped, started the car, and drove out of the parking lot. While driving he pulled his dick out and told me to suck it. Noticing an upcoming red light, I procrastinated until he was at a full stop. I hurried out of the car and took off running until I made it home.

When I entered the door, Hunter was heading out. He could tell something was wrong with me, so he questioned me. I cried as I told him about my experience with Andrew and Sabastian.

When finished he wasted no time responding, "Sis, what the fuck! Those dudes were what you call DL's. They convince everyone they are straight but behind closed doors they are homosexuals. What you went through was risky and you need to go get checked out asap. If they did that to you then no telling how many people they have sex with. If you didn't want to do it, why did you not speak up? You said they were not threatening."

I could not answer Hunter's question because I did not know why I didn't speak up for myself. He made me sit there for several minutes before he said the word fear. He questioned what I was afraid of. Back then I could not explain why, but now I know it was because I was in fear of being rejected.

Since I could not answer for myself, Hunter started making assumptions. He pretty much called it, I had low self-esteem and feared rejection so much that I could not defend myself. His method was taking me to the spot and taught me to cook drugs. I guess his logic was to keep me occupied so I would not end up in the situation I had fallen victim to. He didn't bother to explain why this move was a good one. I caught on fast and a week later I was employed and cooking after school to stay busy. But that only lasted a month because the spot got kicked in. Luckily, it happened right after Hunter took all the drugs to distribute. But there was paraphernalia around and since I was the only one in the house, I was taken to juvenile.

Marshall had his girlfriend India come and get me. You never saw her unless there was something big going on. Marshall protected their relationship. All his other women knew to act like they had sense when India was around. But I knew deep down those women were envious of her and they wanted her position. Instead of finding their own man they would rather waste their time with Marshall in hope the relationship would fall apart. They were just waiting around for a relationship to fail so they could get a chance. I never wanted to be that woman. But who was I to judge because I never had a boyfriend.

When I came out of the family court building Marshall was pissed. We got home and I watched my brothers argue. Hunter finally explained his logic. He was trying to make me street so that I could feel power and build confidence. Jewl agreed with his view and reminded Marshall about what happened with the janitor. Then Hunter, who was on the hotseat, defended Marshall's logic behind the janitor. Like always Jewl saw both sides and the argument was over. They both had made street decisions to help me in a positive way.

It was saddening. These three young men were trying to raise themselves and survive in the world but did not possess the tools to make healthy choices. India stepped in and volunteered to spend more time with me so that I could stay out of trouble.

Moving forward, twice per week I went over to her apartment. She showed me so many new things like art, writing, inspiring movies, and events in the city that I knew nothing about. It was crazy how I was a freshman in high school and the place I had been living all my life I knew nothing about.

I wanted the nice things that India had. She was smart, beautiful, independent, confident, and had money. And even having what seemed to be everything she said she still had goals to be better than she was yesterday. That was our saying "be better than yesterday". Unfortunately, her evolution would be the reason why she broke up with Marshall. Months later, she took a job in another state and wanted him to go but Marshall would not leave because we needed him.

Once again, I had a lot of time on my hands. India would call me about things going on in the city, but I was not motivated to go because she was not with me. I learned that being in a box all my life affected my social skills and being in unfamiliar places increased my anxiety. Scarlett tried to attend some of the places with me when she was not busy running her father's business.

I tried to take Harper with me, but she was too ghetto and uninterested. I told India and she suggested that I get into some programs at school. I found this college accelerated program. I completed one college course per semester and by senior year, I would have credits that can transfer to any college in the country. India suggested I use that opportunity to get my college reading, math, and social sciences out the way. With a plan for my future, I was motivated again.

The more education I got the more I grew apart from my friends. Harper was in a dysfunctional relationship and pregnant. Grace was still on drugs heavy and constantly in and out of jail. I became a loner spending a lot of time at the library when I was not in school. But it was cool because I was reading so many books. I loved urban fiction; my favorite authors were Rosa James, V.C Andrews, Ashley Antoinette, Mary Monroe, Mary B. Morrison, Zane, Walter B. Mosely, Jacquavius Coleman, Carl Weber, and Kwan just to name a few. Reading took me away from the world and helped me forget about the things that were going on inside and around me.

CHAPTER SEVEN

ADVERSITY

I was so wrapped up in my world that I didn't notice that my mother was struggling. She still had not found a job and the bills were piling up. Desperate to change things Marshall, Hunter, and Jewel began strategizing to buy a house. They hustled harder selling drugs, robbing, whatever it took to raise enough money to buy a decent home that could accommodate all of us.

But coming up with at least sixty thousand in a short time called for some desperate measures. We received the eviction notice, and the sheriff was due to put our stuff out on the curb in thirty days. Marshall had to pay the rent up and court costs just to buy us some time, so it put a dent in the money that they were saving to buy a house. Paying up the bills also revealed what my brothers were up to. I remember our mother was upset but she could not do much because the street money was keeping us with a roof over our heads.

I am not sure why they never asked Uncle Clifton for the money. But that was Hunter and Marshall's call. Jewl thought they were crazy but had to honor their request. I figured it was a man thing, so I just stayed out of it and focused on my reading and schoolwork. Although there was a lot of adversity around me during this time, I was living carefree. No one objected to my introvertive behavior because it was safe. But while I was in my carefree world, I had no idea I would be on the chopping block to make some money.

One evening, I was heading to the kitchen to make me something to eat when Jewel approached me. He wanted me to ride with him. Now I needed to question things because the last time one of my brothers told me to get in the car, I witnessed a man die, and I was cooking drugs. I hurried and made a sandwich before we left the house and got into his car. As he drove, he talked to me about how important it was for me not to fall into the cracks of the streets. He said that if I was just so persistent to be weak for some dick then his job was to make me strong.

We parked in front of a shack of a house on the south side of town. I was not familiar with this area because I never ventured beyond 63rd street. All I heard was that southside dudes were crazy and I believed it because Harper's baby's father was from the southside, and he was abusive to her.

We got out of the car and walked up to the front door. My brother knocked three times and a man abruptly opened the door then invited us inside. As I walked past the man, he gave me a lustful stare and I welcomed it because he was cute.

He and my brother went to the kitchen to discuss business while I sat on the couch. The man came out of the kitchen and handed me the remote and told me to make myself at home. I turned on the television and started watching Netflix. He went in the back where I assumed the bedrooms were and came back out with a stack of money and what appeared to be a bag of cocaine.

He sat the money on the table while making the comment, "I see you like to chill and watch movies." He gave me another lustful stare and winked before going back into the kitchen.

Then the loud music started playing and the familiar aroma of crack cooking invaded the air. Jewel came out the kitchen with a scarf wrapped around his face and handed me one. He also handed me a lit blunt and told me we would be gone in another couple hours. The moment he went back into the kitchen, the man came out and boldly slipped me his number. For the next couple hours,

we exchanged flirtatious stares while Jewl stayed

in the kitchen seeming not to notice.

When finished, we left the house and went

straight back home. When I got to my bedroom,

Jewl's girlfriend Luna was in my bed watching

television. We used to be close but after the Grace

incident, I didn't care much for her. But that didn't

stop her from trying to salvage our friendship. She

basically lived in our house and earned her keep by

cleaning, cooking, boosting clothing and

necessities. She even had a food stamp plug, so I

knew she was not going anywhere soon because my

brothers loved to eat. My mother liked her also and

she was the only one that could come and go.

I didn't really want to talk to Luna, but I

didn't have anyone else to talk to, so I confided in

her. She said that southside niggas were wild but

took care of their girls. She said she used to fuck

with one and he would smack her around from time to time, but she didn't want for nothing. She also advised me that I did not need to get too comfortable because Jewl would never have taken me to this man's house without a reason.

A week later, I learned she was right when Jewl tossed me a burner phone and told me to call dude from that phone only. He also had other dummy numbers in the phone that he said would call or text me so it would not seem suspicious.

In less than a week, I was chilling on the man's couch watching movies. I learned his name was Asher and his family originated from New Orleans. Asher was cool as fuck. He was smart and kept me entertained. When I was with him, I stayed high, tipsy, full, laughing, and fucked good. We kept our world a secret because I learned over time, he had a woman. I was his secret, and I was cool with that because we were enjoying each other's company.

I was fifteen and sexually inexperienced, so Asher taught me so many things in the bedroom. But what I loved the most was that we had good conversations about my goals and dreams. He was the reason why I figured out I wanted to be an anesthesiologist.

I was falling for him and started resenting Jewl. Why would he place me in this situation and not expect me to fall for Asher's charm. Weeks went by and I didn't want things to end. I talked to Luna about the situation, and she told me that I had no choice but to stick with my brother when it came to Asher. She told me that it was going to be all good at the beginning, but Asher would throw me away when he got bored and return to his family.

I didn't want to believe that Asher was just fucking me over. Me and Jewl argued for a week straight before I finally told him what he needed to know and that was where the safe was. That night before I went to Asher's, I begged Jewl not to kill him. I asked him was there a way he could just rob Asher and spare his life. Jewl told me that if he left Asher alive then he would put things together and find out anyway.

He made me look in the mirror and question myself. Over the course of the time did Asher ever express wanting a relationship? Did he take me to meet his loved ones or care about meeting mines? And the most important factors, I was underaged and he was secretly fucking a business associates' younger sister so there was no respect or good intention. Jewl encouraged me to get Asher before he got me.

I was restless at Asher's house. He could tell my mood was off, so he inquired. I made up a story about arguing with my mother. Once again Asher gave me good advice before fucking me the best he had ever since we met. At 3:00am Asher had fallen into a deep sleep. I went to the kitchen and unlocked the back door before returning to the bedroom. Later that morning, I awakened and was showering with Asher.

That's when Jewl made his move. He entered the house and went into the bathroom. He made me stay in the shower while he took Asher to the safe to open it. Once the safe was opened, he made him come back to the shower and stand next to me. He instructed me to step out of the shower and when I did, Jewl fired his gun. Asher slid to the floor and died. I watched the water shower his slumped body, washing his leaking blood down the drain.

While Jewl cleaned the safe of drugs and money, I got dressed and removed everything that placed me at his house at any time, even the very sheets we slept on.

We went home and I went straight to my bedroom and laid down. Luna came in and checked on me and I cried. Later that night, I watched the breaking news. Asher's girlfriend came to the house after Asher did not show up to church later that morning. She had a key and when she entered, she found him in the shower dead. The news never disclosed anything about a robbery, and they were looking for tips to solve the homicide.

Jewl came in the bedroom and looked at the television. He sat on my bed and handed me a blunt before saying, "Sis, a nigga's weakness will always be pussy."

CHAPTER EIGHT

UNPRETENTIOUS

Against Jewl's say, I found a way to get to that funeral. I knew it was risky, but I did not care. Yeah, I knew his main chick would be there, but I would have to bear it because I wanted to say goodbye. When I arrived at the church it was already a lot of drama going on. There were literally females fighting each other over Asher. His main chick was escorted out for the safety of herself and her unborn child. Then a shootout broke out outside the church, and everyone began scattering. When the coast was clear, I slipped out a side door and hurried to my mom's car. I drove to a local park and read Asher's obituary.

It's crazy how you don't really love and admire someone until they die. I guess it's because everyone compiles all their accomplishments and good memories into one place for everyone to see. But this obituary was also an opportunity to learn more about who he really was and where he came from. Yeah, we had deep conversations, but Asher was good at not disclosing a lot about himself. He kept the focus on me when he was with me, and I fell for it because I was thirsty for attention and acceptance.

While reading, I just didn't understand why Asher was in the streets so heavily. He was the youngest of seven children and grew up with both parents in the home. He was a Muslim and had a church home. He owned a couple businesses and was on the Community Action Committee with his mother who was into politics. But what broke my heart was that I learned he not only had a baby on the way but had recently proposed to his girlfriend.

On that note, I needed something to numb the pain, so I went to the liquor store in my neighborhood that did not ID. When I got to the store, it was crowded outside as usual. As I passed various groups of people, it seemed like Asher's funeral was the number one topic. After purchasing my items, I was going out the door when I bumped into someone. When I looked up there was the man that was going to take my mind off Asher. It was quick but it was something familiar about him. I felt comfortable like I already knew him. We exchanged numbers and went our separate ways. I didn't bother to ask him his name because he would be the only nigga calling my phone.

A few days later, I was lying in my bed listening to the rain when my cell rang. It was him. He wanted to see me, so I snuck out and met him at the gas station around the corner from my house. No one would notice because my mother was in her bedroom in a drunken sleep and my brothers were still out hustling hard to make the money to remodel the house they had just purchased. We had

Jewl to thank for the lick. Asher had enough money

in his safe to purchase a six-bedroom home fixer

upper for my family and enough drugs for my

brothers to sale to make the money for the

renovations.

I learned that his name was Julian. We went

to a hotel and took shots of tequila while talking all

night. He was cool to be around. He reeled me in

with his personality and overtime his consistency.

Julian had my nose wide open. I thought about him

every day and night. I even had dreams about him.

When we were not together, I was afraid that

someone else was getting the love and attention he

was giving me. I remember sitting around creating

scenarios in my mind of what he could be doing

and what I would do if I caught him. He had the

insecurity seeping out of my pours. I learned later

that's what he needed to see so he could manipulate me.

As time went by, I stopped focusing on my schoolwork. It was all about Julian. I found myself trying to prove to him that I was a down-ass chick, and he took full advantage of that.

It started with me helping him distribute drugs. Then he had me snorting coke with him and drinking. I started staying away from home for days at a time. Then he convinced me to leave my cell at home and come with him. He said that my brothers would never accept our relationship, so he helped me hide from them. Kansas City was small so I knew eventually we would have to see them. But for that moment, Julian suggested we build our relationship so that we could show them we were solid when the time came.

That's when he took me to the place he called home. I felt special that he finally trusted me. We drove there at night, and I got lost in between the twists, turns, and dead-end streets. Honestly, I could not tell you if I was in Missouri or Kansas. We parked inside the garage before getting out of the car and going inside. He gave me a grand tour starting at the lower level that consisted of a bedroom, family room, kitchenette, and full bathroom. When I noticed the stripper pole in the middle of the family room. Julian told me that he did a lot of entertaining. We went upstairs to the main level where he showed me his guest bedrooms, living room, dining area, and kitchen. He saved the master bedroom for last.

Weeks went by and I had completely forgotten about my family. I was in a dream literally because I was high all the time. We fucked every day; I wanted to have his baby. But God did not allow a pregnancy because he knew what was best. Then in the blink of an eye things started to change. Julian became more demanding after my sixteenth birthday. He made me wear lingerie all the time even in front of his homies. I tried to stay inside the bedroom so they would not see me, but he would find reasons to call me out. One night after seeing his homies out, he came upstairs and laid on the bed next to me. I was high and feeling playful, so I started dancing for him. He seemed interested as he gripped my winding hips. All that good cooking he was doing was thickening me up in all the right places. He told me that he wanted me to strip on the pole downstairs. We hurried down and he turned on R-Kelly. I got on the pole and went to work like a pro. When you fall for a man it's so easy to do any and everything he wants you to do.

While I danced, I imagined I was in the movie "The Players Club". He sat on the couch in a trance and that made me go harder. I got creative and started taking off my clothes. Naked, I clapped

my ass and spread my legs. I exposed it all for my

man. He rose from the couch, and we had the most

intense sex in the middle of the floor. When

finished, he went over to a video camera and

turned it off. I could not believe it! He had been

recording me the whole time. I began yelling

because I knew what happened with the videos. My

brothers used to record females all the time and sit

around watching with their homies.

But Julian said this was not that; I was his

woman, and this is what couples did. He made me

sit down and watch the video. Then we had sex

again. I trusted his word and the camera became a

part of our bedroom. While I was thinking we were

keeping things spicy, I learned that Julian was

sharing our intimate moments with his homies. I

confronted him about it one night and he laughed

in my face. He said his boys are solid and would not

tell a soul. I believed him. He had a way of convincing me that things were all good.

But I learned to never get too comfortable with Julian. One night, he came into the room and told me that he needed me to start pulling my weight if I wanted to be with him forever. He said that his bitch had to get money by any means and if I could not be that person I had to go. I didn't want to leave him. I remembered Luna telling me that to keep a man you had to put in work and do whatever they needed you to do. She said that was the price of being a kept woman.

I thought he was going to have me selling drugs again, or even find a job but that was far from the case. Days later, I was dancing on the pole in front of his homeboys and a few other men I never seen before. This shit went down every night, but the reward was Julian counting the money in front of me at the end of the night.

He said I was holding it down and he was proud of me. But over time, he took it to the next level. This is when the pimping started. His close associates came to the house to have sex with me, and strangers met up at local motels. This went on for months. The only time my vagina could rest was when I was on my menstrual. But there was always something to do during that time like dancing or sucking dick.

Time passed and Julian kept taking it up a notch. I was participating in threesomes and fulfilling strange fetishes. These duties required more drugs because to slip a dildo in a man's ass, I needed to numb myself.

All these different men having their way with my body caused me immeasurable pain. A shower seemed to never be enough to wash away all the strangers that were inside of me. Julian wasn't having sex with me anymore; I didn't blame him because who would want to lay up with a woman that fucked and sucked strangers every day.

I wanted out but didn't know how to get away. I was falling deeper into my suffering and became depressed. I tried to kill myself in the bathtub one night, but Julian came in just in time. He said I was weak, and he had no time for suicide watch. He locked me in the bedroom, and I laid there depressed thinking about Asher.

Julian did not care about my depression. He was sending men up to the bedroom to fuck me as I laid there in a trance. They must have been complaining about my lack of participation because Julian really started treating me bad. He would verbally abuse me all day. He controlled when I ate and showered. He even made me stand in a corner of the room like I was in time out for hours.

One night, I overheard one of his homies say that I was becoming dead weight, and it was time to get rid of me. I thought I was going to die that night, but I didn't care about life anymore. Julian came to the bedroom and told me that I had a customer waiting at a motel. On this night, things were different because usually Julian waited in the car watching the door. But he dropped me off and said he would return when I was finished. I looked at my watch and it read 3:00am. At this point, I knew I needed to pay attention because something always happened at this time. I entered the room expecting the worse but to my surprise, the stranger was Mateo, Jewl's friend. He was just as shocked to see me than I was he. With no questions he took me straight home to my brothers.

Once again, I was at the table explaining how fucked up things were to them. I could tell Jewl was uncomfortable, so I did not disclose anything about Asher. Later that night, Jewl came to my bedroom to drop a bombshell on me. He said Julian was Asher's half-brother on his father's side. Asher's parents were happily married but had their flaws and Julian was that. He was not in the obituary because Asher's mother forbade it.

But Julian and Asher had established their own relationship outside the family and were close. Julian was the one that pulled Asher into the streets because he envied his brother's perfect life. He said Julian knew who I was the whole time. He made me swear that I never revealed to Marshall and Hunter that I was involved in Asher's setup. But Days later things got worse. Julian was showing the video footage and photos of my naked ass all over the city. Our secret was not safe any longer when Julian waged war against Jewl for killing Asher. That was the first time I had ever seen my brothers physically fight each other and it was all because of me.

I felt so guilty because my actions were sabotaging my family even more. I learned that while I was away, my mother started doing drugs. Marshall was able to send her away to rehab. He planned to have the house ready by the time she got out and we were leaving the inner city. While waiting, I spent most of my days in my bedroom hiding from the world. I was so embarrassed. I missed a lot of my junior year but the college program I was in was dual credits, so I only had to make up one semester for my junior year to catch up.

India was living in Canada, but she contacted my school and was able to pull some strings for my assignments to be completed at home. Faithfully, every Monday Marshall picked up my assignments and dropped off the completed ones every Friday afternoon.

In that bedroom alone, I tried to do a lot of soul searching. Meanwhile my brothers were going through it. Julian had proven to be a menace, constantly taunting them. They were having gun battles, getting robbed, and ultimately the house we lived in was shot up. The landlord came that night and told us we had to go especially after finding out my mother was in rehab. We went out to Uncle Clifton's for the next couple months until the house was finished.

When my senior year started, my mother was out of rehab, we were moved into our new home, and I was going to a new school. Since my grades were good, India was able to get me some scholarships into private school. It was like pressing the reset button on my life. I was in a new place gaining new friends and I could leave my past behind. I stayed away from social media and out of the inner city. The goal was to graduate and go to

college.

CHAPTER NINE

EMBARKATION

I made it through my senior year without any issues. Harper and I reconnected, and she was pregnant with her third child. We made weekly visits to Grace who was still incarcerated. Hunter ended up getting locked up and was due to be released the following year. Jewl was still heavy in the streets; his ego would not allow him to stop. He was determined to get back at Julian no matter what the cost was.

I wanted to stay around my friends so against India's wishes, I decided to go to college from home. It seemed like things had died down and I could live a normal life if I stayed out the inner city. Mateo was able to stop the circulation of the video and pictures because I was a minor, but the people that saw it would never allow me to forget.

Uncle Clifton started coming around more often and being the father figure I needed. Marshall did not care much for Uncle Clifton's presence, but he didn't trip because it was better than no one being around. He had gone off to college and had plans to move to Canada with India; she was pregnant with his daughter.

It was finally time to plan my graduation party. I was so happy because I had never had a party. It seemed to always be something going on whenever my birthday came around every year, so I was determined to have a graduation celebration. Our yard was big enough for friends from my school to come. My mother was excited for me.

Harper and I stayed up to 3:00am making the final touches to the plans. My mother had prepared the guest bedroom, but Harper insisted on going home.

God always has a plan and no matter what you do nothing can detour it. Harper loved our house and practically lived with us. That was my mother's way of making up for what happened with Grace. She promised me that she would never turn Grace or Harper away because they were family. But this night, Harper went home with plans to return the next day. I knew she was trying to go be with her baby daddy.

I helped her bundle the babies up and we secured them in their seats. That hug she gave me resided with me. The way she said I love you affected me differently that night. It was like the universe was telling me this was the last goodbye. I remember I watched her drive down the street until I could not see her lights anymore. She never texted me to let me know she made it home that night. I figured she made it home and got wrapped up in getting the kids to bed so she forgot.

The next morning, I texted her good morning as I always did, and she did not respond. I dismissed it and went to school, but when she went almost the whole day without texting me, I got worried.

It was my last day of class. When I got home, I was going to tell my mom to take me to the inner city to check on her. When I came in the front door, my mother was sitting on the couch with a cigarette in one hand and a bottle of wine in the other. I knew I was going to receive bad news because she had stopped smoking and drinking. Then the words came out of her mouth. Harper and her children were dead. High off PCP, her baby's father killed them all before turning the gun on himself.

The next day, Uncle Clifton and my mother took me to the jail to break the news to Grace. Marshall paid for the funeral and my mother planned it. Watching my friend lay in the coffin with a deceased child on each side of her and one in her belly was unexplainable.

After that, back to the bedroom I went. I was numb and refused to attend my graduation. This could not be my life so full of pain and trauma. Everyone around me was failing. Harper and her babies dead. Grace snapped and killed an inmate and was given more time. Hunter was in solitary confinement so much he was losing his mind. Jewl was in the streets heavy, and it was only a matter of time before he ended up dead or in prison.

Things were so dark, shit I should have just snorted some coke and relapsed like my mother. Uncle Clifton managed to talk me out of the bedroom the day of my graduation. He said it was up to me to make something happen in all this adversity. He pointed out that it was the reason why I was experiencing so many things in such a short time. He said if it was not meant for me to make it then I would have been dead or in prison.

I went to that ceremony and held back tears while I thought about Harper and her babies. When the ceremony was over, Jewl, Aunt Renee, and Uncle Clifton were waiting for me in the parking lot. Some of my classmates wanted me to go out but I declined. I just wanted to go back home and grieve for my friend. Like the principle said, tomorrow was a new day and I had to figure it out.

When I made it to the parking lot, Aunt Renee approached me. She gave me a hug and said, "I love you so much and I am proud of you." When she released her embrace and looked at me there were tears in her eyes.

At this point I did not have time for the games, I needed to know what was wrong now. It had to be my mother because she was not at the graduation.

I was not prepared to learn that Marshall was killed on the way to the graduation. I fell to my knees and screamed for my brother. Jewl had to carry me to the car. When I made it home, my mother was on the couch waiting. When I looked at her, I didn't see sadness but rage. She charged me and began beating me while screaming it's all your fault.

Julian killed my brother. I ran to my bedroom with no plans on ever coming out. Hours later, Uncle Clifton and Aunt Renee came to check on me. He handed me a one-way plane ticket to Houston, Texas and told me to pack a small bag because I was leaving in a few hours. He said he had everything already set up for me and someone would be waiting at the airport. I refused to go, I had to attend my brother's funeral.

Then Jewl came into the room and said I wasn't staying. They took me to the airport. Before I got on the plane, I looked back at my family one last time.

Jewl mouthed the words, "I love you and I am sorry."

On that plane ride, I looked out the window thinking about all the pain I caused by making bad decisions. Everything that happened seemed to revolve around the result of something I did.

Assad, I have been carrying that guilt for years.

Yellow was the color of the panties I was wearing when my Uncle Elon tried to rape me. I wake up at 3:00am every morning because I saw a man die and it was the last time I saw Harper and her children alive. It also represents when Mateo saved me and when I arrived in Texas to start a new life. The emptiness in my eyes are the what ifs. I ask myself the same things every day.

What if, I would have told that counselor that I was raped in the janitor's closet.

What if I would have gone to the authorities and told them what happened with Sebastian and Andrew.

What if I never went with Jewl to Asher's house that night.

What if my mother let Grace stay with us.

What if Harper never went home that night.

What if I stood up for myself.

What if my mother protected me when Uncle Elon tried to molest me.

Chaya screamed and cried all the years of pain, embarrassment, confusion, poor decisions that made her feel less of a woman. Assad held her tight. He would stay by her side until the last tear dropped because he loved her.

When she reached her final cries, Assad placed his hand under her chin and lifted her head. He stared into her eyes while speaking, "Chaya, you are right. Your past does change how I feel about you. But not the way you think. It makes me love and appreciate you more. All the trauma you endured, and you still did not give up. You know how many people are not able to rise above their past issues and find a good quality of life. You are a fighter, the type of woman I want by my side. Don't hold your head down in shame of the choices you made because you persevered and broke many cycles. If anything, you are the hero of your family. Your scars may hurt but they are a badge of honor, and you have a powerful testimony. You are my queen." Assad kneeled on one knee and opened the black box displaying the diamond ring.

"Chaya, will you marry me now."

Chaya was in shock. After what she told him, this man still wanted her to be his wife. She looked at the clock, it was 6:00am. Assad was still on one knee waiting for the answer. Chaya watched the sun rise before looking down at Assad. "Yes, I will marry you."

Later that day during sunset Assad married his queen. No need for preparation, no need for an audience. Just two people displaying true love, willing to sacrifice and accept each other's flaws. So never feel you are not worthy enough because of your past.

WHAT IF

CHAPTER TEN

SORRY

Chaya sat in the restaurant with Assad waiting for her mother to arrive. She felt nauseated and was not sure if it was nervousness or the baby growing in her womb.

"I ordered you some tea to settle your stomach," said Assad.

Chaya offered a weak smile. She appreciated him so much for going above and beyond. Months ago after the wedding, Chaya started seeing the therapist Assad suggested. It felt good getting things off her chest, but to continue her path of true healing and closure she had to do the work and face her past. Chaya needed to understand why her mother did not protect her.

As the waiter placed the tea on the table, Ginger entered. She looked around until she spotted her daughter. When Chaya looked up and saw her mother, she began trembling.

Assad placed his hands on hers and whispered, "Don't worry. Everything will be fine."

When Ginger made it to the table, Chaya stood and greeted her with a brief hug before returning to her seat. "Momma, this is Assad, my husband."

"Nice to finally meet you," greeted Assad, pulling out a chair for Ginger to take a seat. "I will be in the cigar lounge watching the game. If you ladies need anything, just holla."

Chaya watched Assad disappear into the lounge before focusing back to her mother who was displaying a not so welcoming look.

"Husband! I did not receive any news of this. And a baby?" Ginger pointed to Chaya's pudge.

Chaya could feel a lump forming in her throat. It would be easier to just get up and walk away like she had done years ago by moving to another state. But she made a promise to herself that she would do the work so she could truly move forward and be the best wife and mother she could be. Her cell phone vibrated. When she checked her phone, it was a text message from Assad: *Just take a breath, you got this.*

She placed the phone down and took a breath.

Ginger could tell her daughter was nervous. "Seems like you have something heavy to get off your chest. I have not seen or heard from you in years." She waved the waiter over and ordered a frozen Margarita.

When the waiter walked away, Chaya spoke, "Mother, I realized a lot of my past traumas still affect me in the present. I don't want to bring a baby into the world with all this toxicity, so I made the decision to come back home and get closure and it starts with you."

Ginger looked back for the waiter; she knew she needed to be tipsy for whatever conversation Chaya was going to have with her. "Look, Chaya, I know I worked a lot, relapsed occasionally, and we struggled. I am sorry about that. But I did the best I could with what I had."

"Momma, it's not the struggle or the fact that you worked a lot that affects me. It's why you did not help me when I needed you. When Uncle Elon tried to molest me, you did not console me, it was like you dismissed it. You were still the best with Uncle Elon like you did not care that he did this to me. I hated myself because I was convinced you did not care about what happened. I suffered and made a lot of poor decisions from that one trauma alone. I stopped trusting you and when other things happened to me, I did not tell you because I did not think you would protect me. Then the final straw was when you blamed me for Marshall's death."

The waiter came over and sat the drink on the table. Chaya thanked him and focused back to her mother who was now staring out the window. Ginger cradled her face to catch the tears that ran from her eyes. This was the reason why her daughter never came back home. Throughout their childhood, Ginger assumed her children were okay because things appeared to be good. The house was always clean when she came home from work, they all got good grades. Everyone seemed happy.

"Momma, I am not here to punish you. I just want to understand why." Chaya placed her hand on her mother's.

Ginger focused on the diamond wedding ring. "I can tell that man loves you by the size of that diamond. I am so grateful that you found someone to love you because you deserve it. Chaya, there is so much to say, and I just don't know how."

"Just tell me the truth. How did you feel? What held you back? I will still love you, but this could give me understanding on why things happened the way they did," encouraged Chaya.

Assad approached the table. "I was able to reserve the private dining area for you two."

"Thank you, Assad, you seem like a true gentleman," said Ginger, standing up and grabbing her margarita from the table. Both Chaya and her mother followed Assad to the room.

"I ordered all the appetizers on the menu and don't worry, Ms. Ginger, you have bottomless margaritas." Assad walked away returning to the cigar lounge.

"Wow, he is on top of things," said Ginger, taking a seat.

Chaya sat down, grabbed a saucer, and began placing different items on it realizing she had not eaten all day. Assad always filled in the blanks for her. She wanted to be able to give him that exceptional support like she had done when they first met.

Ginger continued, "I understand why you need this now. You have a king on your hands, and you want to make sure you can be the queen he needs."

Chaya nodded while chewing her food. Ginger took a few sips of her drink. Reaching into her past and facing her truth was going to be difficult because it was all ugly. But if this was her chance to help her daughter, she would go through the pain to prove her love as a mother.

She had already experienced so much pain with her boys. Marshall's death, and Hunter suffered from mental illness from incarcerations and other traumas he would not disclose. Jewl was still in the streets trying to maintain his older brother's legacy. He had done a lot of dirt and was living on borrowed time. Ginger needed Chaya to succeed because that would validate that she did not completely fail as a mother.

"Chaya, when I was eleven, I was molested by one of my uncles. I went and told my mother, and she slapped me and told me to never say anything about it again. Months later, I went to my father, and I learned fast that was the worst move I could have made because he started raping me and your Aunt Lane. He would come into our room what seemed to be every night. Why didn't my mother question him in our room so late in the dark? Then Lane ended up pregnant and he made my mother send her to a private school with nuns where she gave birth and was forced to put the baby up for adoption.

While Lane was away, I was left at the mercy of my father and uncle. I met the boys' father Akeem. He was in a gang and sold drugs, but he offered a sanctuary from the abuse. I would sneak out almost every night but that did not help. I began running away for days, sometimes weeks at a time. When I found out I was pregnant with Marshall, I thought I was safe, but I was wrong.

Akeem went to jail, and I had to take my boys back home. My father was dealing with some health issues, so it prevented him from raping me, but that did not stop him from catching fills.

As for my uncle, he met the love of his life and was so interested in her he no longer bothered me. Lane returned home and things were sort of normal except she struggled with drugs and alcohol to numb the pain of her trauma.

We hated our mother and father, but we had to be obedient because that's how it was during our time. No matter what your parents or loved ones did, you had to love them and respect them based on their title. Staying with a family was more important than addressing trauma. You never talked about things that were wrong, you just swept it under the rug and prayed for a better day. As time passed, I started to get comfortable again and that's when my uncle raped me again. Nine months later, I gave birth to you.

I never told anyone, not even my sister. Akeem got out of jail. When he found out I had a baby he was sure I cheated. He took the boys out of anger. Having a baby by my uncle was embarrassing. I could not tell him what really happened for years. When I finally did, he wanted to kill my uncle and take us away. He said he would be your father, and no one ever had to know anything different. But I protected my family and for that I sabotaged our relationship.

I remember Akeem's exact words, "What type of sick bitch sits at the dinner table with the men who have raped her all her life?"

Well, I didn't know how to be strong and face them because they were my family and my mother said family had to stick together.

So, it was just me and you in the house. I started working to try and get out but since my father was sick my mother was taking a lot of my money. The older you got the more you started to resemble your father and Lane began to question. When I confessed, she was furious.

That night, we had a family meeting. It was me, Lane, my parents, uncle, and Elon. My sister and I tried to tell my mother everything again in front of everyone. Maybe she would react differently if she knew that the sexual abuse was continuing, and more offenders were involved. My father denied his wrongdoing and my mother defended him. But my uncle apologized to both me and my sister. He took full accountability and promised to never violate us again.

At this point my mother was crying. She would not look either one of us in the eyes. Lane would not accept our uncle's apology. She even threatened to tell the love of his life what he had done.

Then our father started being a complete asshole and smacked Lane. He said that if we didn't wear such provocative clothing then the men would not be tempted. In rage, Lane tried to fight our father back, she had the advantage because he was weak. Our mother rose from her seat and grabbed my sister and told her she should never raise her hand to her father. In shock, Lane backed away slowly. She had had enough. She looked at me and reached out her hand. She said we could go and get help. They had shelters we could live in until we got on our feet. She promised that she would stay with me and help take care of you. Why didn't I take her hand and walk out that front door? When Lane realized I would not go, life seemed to drain from her eyes. She dropped her hand and barged out the front door.

She was gone for weeks, and I needed her home to take care of you while I worked. I trusted you in the care of your Uncle Elon. He was in high school during that time, so he watched you in the evenings and overnight. One night, I got off work early. When I got home, I found you asleep in Elon's bed with no pamper on.

At that moment, I went crazy and began beating Elon waking him from his sleep. My mother came into the room and began beating me in his defense. I yelled at her telling her what I found. That woman looked me dead in my eyes and said that nothing was happening. She said that you started taking off your own pampers, and that meant it was time to start potty training you. She picked up the pamper on the side of the bed and tossed it at me.

Elon pleaded with me that he would never do such a thing and I fell for it. That morning I went out and found Lane and begged her to come home. She agreed to come back and help me take care of you. But she was on drugs bad. To keep her around, I would feed her drug habit. Years went by and things seemed to go back to normal, but we still battled with the scars. Then I found out that your Uncle Elon tried to touch you. My parents seemed to be handling the situation because they sent him away. But when he returned, I was done.

Lane could no longer take it; she told me that if I did not leave with her that night, I would never see her again. I wish I could have gone with her because that night she committed suicide. She was found two days later inside her car at a local park. Your uncle Clifton and his wife invited me to move with them to their new home. I moved out and only returned to help my parents who were sick.

Years later, I had enough money saved to move into a place. Akeem and I got back together. We were a family now and I just wanted to forget about everything. So, I buried it and walked around numb. But Akeem could not stand that I was still supporting the family that was abusing me and caused the death of my sister.

We began arguing almost every day. I was so fucked up in the head and had normalized the abuse. I still defended my family. He could not take it and left us all and questioned if the boys really belonged to him. He demanded a DNA test, but I was afraid to do it because what if the boys really were not his.

Chaya, all of this is the reason why I did not properly protect you. I was weak, traumatized, confused, and for that, I am sorry.

CHAPTER ELEVEN

THE ROOT OF THE TRAUMA

Four margaritas in, Ginger explained to her daughter the best way she could why she was not the best mother. While listening, Chaya could not help but wonder which uncle violated her mother. All her great uncles were in and out of prison and out of town except for Uncle Clifton.

"Who is my father?" questioned Chaya.

Ginger allowed more tears to fall before answering, "Uncle Clifton."

Chaya rose from the table and ran out. She went into the powder room and locked herself inside. She looked in the mirror at herself. The layers were all peeled away to the toxic seeds that had dictated her life. Uncle Clifton had been her only hero. He taught her everything she knew and kept in touch with her. He was the reason why she was able to get through college. He did everything that at father should do for his daughter.

To learn that the man she looked up to was one of the reasons why she suffered for years was a new trauma she had to deal with. She felt disgusted and wished at that moment she would just drop dead. Assad knocked on the door. When Chaya did not answer, he instructed the owner to unlock it.

When he entered, Chaya charged him and began hitting him while yelling, "Why did you make me do this?"

Assad grabbed her wrist firmly and tried to calm her down. He looked into her eyes. "I did this because I love you and I did not want you to continue to rot from the inside out from your trauma." His voice was authoritative, but gentle. He hugged Chaya while she cried, releasing years of pain and frustration.

"I am a product of incest; this is so embarrassing. Why didn't my mom abort me?" spoke Chaya her voice low.

"But you are perfectly healthy. Remember Clifton is your grandmother's half-brother. No matter what, we are going to be okay," answered Assad.

Chaya backed away from him. "I don't deserve you because I am flawed. What if something is wrong with the baby? You know sometimes things skip generations."

"We will handle whatever comes our way because I love you," responded Assad.

"No! Love is not enough! I have too many problems. Assad, you deserve a woman that has her shit at least halfway together and that is not me. After I give birth to our son, I will sign all my rights over to you and we will divorce. I want you to find a woman that can be the best wife and mother to our child because it's not me."

Assad pulled her back into his embrace. "No, I love you and we deserve each other."

Chaya broke the embrace. "Assad, I am not going back to California with you. You will not see me until I have this baby, then we will go our separate ways." She went to the sink and began splashing water onto her face. When she looked up, Assad was still standing there and the pain in his eyes was evident.

He spoke in the calmest tone, "I am not agreeing to a divorce. You are my queen and I love all parts of you, both good and bad. I will continue to pray for us and our families. I believe we all can heal and build a family that Assad Jr. deserves."

Chaya looked over noticing her mother standing in the doorway. "Baby, don't let your trauma dictate your life like it did mines. I can't turn back time and I am sorry. But today, I want to start healing with you so that I can be the best grandma to my grandchild. Please don't give up."

"Take me to Aktober's," Chaya demanded. She exited the powder room.

Ginger handed Assad a card with her cell phone number on it. "Don't worry, I will look after her and keep you updated." She left him standing in the powder room alone.

The drive to Aktober's house was quiet. Chaya looked out the window at the familiar places she had left behind. There were very few good memories, and she hated this place, but it was where she belonged. Assad texted her to tell her he loved her, and he hoped she would be on the plane with him in the next forty-eight hours to go back home to California. Chaya tossed the phone back into her bag and continued looking out the window.

"Chaya, please don't punish Assad. I punished Akeem for my trauma and lost him," said Ginger.

"Where did Akeem go?" questioned Chaya.

"He moved to Texas, got married, and started a new family. He started communicating with us again after Marshall died," responded Ginger. She parked in the driveway behind Aktober's car.

They did not get a chance to get out before Aktober ran out in a frantic way. "Ginger, move your car. I have to get over to dad's house."

"Get inside, I will take you," insisted Ginger.

Chaya looked over at her; if looks could kill her mother would be dead.

"You said you wanted to stay here because you deserve it. Well, here you go, Chaya," reminded Ginger.

A few minutes later, they arrived at Uncle Clifton's house. Jewl was sitting outside on the front steps. When he saw Chaya exit the car, he hurried over to her. "Sis, I haven't seen you in the flesh in years." He gave her a hug. The smell of marijuana made Chaya feel sick to her stomach.

"Be careful holding her tight like that, there is a baby baking inside of her," said Ginger before following Aktober.

Once Ginger and Aktober were inside, Jewl looked at his sister and spoke, his tone serious, "Why the fuck are you back here? I told you to never come back, especially carrying my nephew. Leaving this shit behind was the plan." Chaya gave him a questioning look. How did he know she was having a boy.

"I know but leaving this place did not help me heal from my past. I only buried it, and buried things can be unburied. I had to come back for understanding and closure. Plus, I don't want to shut out all my family. But now I feel like I belong here after what momma just told me."

"What the fuck you mean belong here? Just imagine where you would have been if you would have stayed here. What did she tell you?" questioned Jewl.

"Uncle Clifton is my father. He raped momma and I was conceived. Momma was also raped by her father along with Aunt Lane and that's why she killed herself."

Jewel was lost for words.

Suddenly, they heard screaming from inside the house. They hurried inside. When they entered the family room, Aktober was hovering over her father's dead body on the hospital bed. When she saw Chaya, she reached out her hand. "Cousin, your favorite uncle is gone." When Chaya did not move, Aktober surveyed the room. Why was no one sad like her. "My dad is lying here dead, and I am the only one in here shedding tears? All the shit he has done for everyone standing here."

Chaya spoke up, "Aktober, he was a rapist. He raped my mother and got her pregnant. I am his daughter. We are sisters."

In rage, Aktober got to her feet and lunged for Chaya, but Ginger jumped in her path. "From this point moving forward, no one else is ever hurting my daughter as long as I am breathing."

Aktober backed away while speaking, "Y'all really believe my father raped Ginger and got her pregnant. If he was your rapist, why did you live with us? Why did you continue to accept money from him all these years? No one ever stopped you from coming through that front door and sharing a meal with the man that raped you."

"She didn't know how to handle it, just like you didn't know how to handle it," said Hunter, entering the family room. He placed his arm around Chaya and kissed her on the forehead.

"Shut the fuck up, Hunter. Your crazy ass don't know shit. Go find your medicine," said Aktober through gritted teeth.

"It's true. Whenever I came over, Uncle Clifton used to make Aktober and I do fucked up shit with each other when we were children. After she got her period, he made me take her virginity. Uncle Clifton was a sick man. He used to make us watch porn. Then when Aktober turned sixteen he stopped making us do it. I later learned that it was because he started having sex with you."

"Hunter, stop the lies please!" yelled Aktober, now standing in his face.

Renee stepped up. "No, Aktober, you stop the lies. Clifton confessed everything to me. He raped Lane and Ginger. He is Chaya's father and he made Hunter and you do things as children before he started having sex with you. It's all true from his mouth. He had me video it just in case no one believed me."

"Fuck all of you! This was my daddy and he loved me. He needed me when Renee was sick. My daddy told me it was okay because that's what women had to do. He said he was preparing me to make my future husband happy. I still love him." Aktober rested her head at the foot of her father's bed and cried.

"Do you really think that was the reason? Aktober, you can't even keep a man in your life," said Jewl.

The conversation was interrupted by Elon entering. He hurried over to his uncle. "Damn, Unc, I see you when I get there." He placed his hand on Aktober's back; she jerked away.

"Yeah, in hell," fired Ginger. She picked up a vase from the table and hit Elon over the head, shattering it. He fell to the floor and in a flash, Ginger was on top of him holding a pocketknife to his neck. "Elon, did you molest Chaya as a baby?"

"Yeah, tell the truth because Uncle Clifton already confessed his sins before he died," said Jewl.

Ginger pressed the knife to his skin just enough to draw blood. Elon began to cry. "Yes, I did, but I am sorry. I could not control myself. I am fucked up and I didn't want to be like this. But I watched our father and uncle do it for years, so I thought it was okay. My mother didn't care. We used to do things. She said it was okay because she loved me, and it was our secret."

"Fuck! How far does this sick shit go back!" yelled Jewl. He ignored the no smoking policy, pulled out his blunt and lit it.

Generational curses of sexual abuse that goes back to slave owners raping our women and men. Our people being silenced and accustomed to toxic behaviors that were passed down from generation to generation instead of being addressed appropriately. Families were so wrapped up in protecting their bloodline that abusers were able to thrive and continue violating, leaving their victims traumatized. Because who was going to make them accountable? The victims are left with the trauma and its side effects. They rarely find closure, so they numb themselves as they sit across the dinner table from their abuser. They have rage and display promiscuous behaviors. The victim does not feel protected nor trust and inside there is self-hate.

Sometimes the trauma affects the victim so badly that they can't hide it no matter how pretty they package themselves. Assad saw a pretty package at the beginning but began to witness Chaya's trauma eating her from the inside out. The moral to the story is TALK ABOUT IT! DON'T ALLOW YOUR ABUSER TO CONTROL YOUR LIFE. GO TO THERAPY.

Parents get help for your traumas so that you can teach and protect your children. BREAK THE CYCLE OF SEXUAL ABUSE!

Usually, the abuser has been abused. Unresolved sexual trauma can also create predators. That's why it's important that when children display signs of abuse, they need help and protection; not to be condemned and their trauma covered up. Chaya's trauma stemmed from her grandparents, and it was likely they were sexually abused. Just something to think about.

CHAPTER TWELVE

ACCEPT, HEAL, UNITE

Assad sat on the couch in his living room watching television. Months passed since he heard from Chaya, and he prayed every day for a healthy family for his son to thrive in.

Hungry, he went into the kitchen to the fridge. Before opening the door, he looked at the calendar. Chaya was due to deliver their son in two weeks. He opened the fridge and grabbed the left-over Chinese food and put it inside the microwave.

Suddenly, there was a knock at the front door. Assad was not expecting anyone. When he opened it, there stood Chaya, Ginger, Jewl, Hunter, and Renee.

Jewl was holding two grocery bags. He invited himself inside while speaking, "I'm Jewl,

your brother-in-law. I finally got her back to you."
Jewl headed in the direction of the kitchen.

Hunter stepped into the doorway. "I am
Hunter, it's an honor to meet you." He extended his
hand and shook Assad's before following Jewl.

Ginger stepped in the door and embraced
Assad. "Thank you for loving my daughter at one of
her worse times. It was a rough road, but we were
able to get her back to you like I promised." She and
Renee headed to the kitchen to assist Jewl who was
preparing dinner.

Chaya stood in the doorway staring at
Assad. Although her family had invited themselves
inside, she was still not sure that Assad would
receive her again.

"How do you feel?" Assad inquired.

Chaya stepped inside the doorway. Assad
took her hands into his. Chaya looked into his eyes.
"I feel like your wife and the mother of your child. I

want to tell you everything that happened over the past few months."

Assad closed the gap and kissed Chaya on the lips. He placed one of his hands on her protruding belly and his son gave him a strong kick. "You're right, you are my wife, queen, and the mother of my child. I love you. Welcome home." He pulled her completely inside the house and closed the door.

Over dinner everyone took turns explaining what transpired over the past few months. The day following Uncle Clifton's funeral, his lawyer met with everyone. Uncle Clifton owned several commercial and residential properties and stocks. His estate was worth 20 million dollars and he willed it to everyone with instructions to split everything equally. With a new start, everyone decided to leave Kansas City, so they sold all the property and cashed in all the stocks. They split the

money down the middle among all seven of them.
Aktober and Elon wanted nothing to do with the
family, so they went to Georgia. Jewl, Hunter,
Chaya, Ginger, and Renee decided to stick together
and traveled to Texas so that Jewl and Hunter could
reunite with their father.

While in Texas, the family started the path
of healing together. They started both group and
individual therapy. Moving forward, they made a
vow to break the cycle and create a healthier
foundation.

After dinner, Assad's father and
grandmother came over to meet Chaya's family.
Everyone sat in the family room watching
television, playing cards and conversating with
each other.

There was a knock at the front door. When
Assad got up to go answer, his father stopped him,
insisting he would get it. Assad sat back in his seat

and continued his football debate with Hunter. Moments later, someone tapped him on the shoulder. When he turned, his mother was standing there. It had been years since he saw her, but he would never forget her beautiful eyes.

His father said, "Son, I am sorry that I was so hurt that I kept you away from your mother. When you told me about what Chaya was going through and how you were supporting her, I had to look in the mirror. Although your trauma is not the same magnitude as Chaya's, taking your mother away was still something that affected you. To watch this family rise from what happened to them, I knew it was time for me to take some accountability and do what was right for our family so that we can all unite and provide Assad Jr. with the love and support he will need in this world."

Assad was in tears and a weight was lifted from his chest. He had learned to manage not having his mother around over the years and forgave his father for his mistake. But he only locked that pain away and won the battles against the triggers after he was accused of rape. But being able to release it was a breath of fresh air and he owed it all to prayer and belief.

Chaya wrapped her arm around him. "Baby, look at the family that will welcome our son." She reached up to wipe his tears. "I love you, my king." She backed away so that Assad could hug his mother.

Hunter tapped his glass of lemonade. "Okay, now this calls for a toast!" When everyone raised their glasses, he continued, "Let's toast to all the healing that has happened in this room. Let's toast to Assad Jr. who will be coming into a family that will be able to love, protect, support, and teach him. To Assad Jr., the Lion."

THE END

More Books by Rosa James

At

Passion2right.com

About the Author

Rosa James was born in Kansas City Missouri.

She was raised by her maternal grandparents until she was placed into foster care at age eleven. She was later adopted at age fourteen.

Rosa recognized her passion to write at an early age. It started with journaling and freestyling short stories to her friends and family.

She became an avid reader when a relative gave her the book titled 'Petals on the Wind' by V.C Andrews. The fiction drama piqued her interest. She began reading more and was inspired by authors Walter Mosley, Mary Monroe, Mary B. Morrison, Kwan, Ashley, and JaQuavis just to name a few.

In her late teens Rosa wanted to write a book about her life. But later in her mid-twenties decided to start with fiction. However, during that time being a single parent, focusing on a better career, lack of education and resources posed obstacles.

In the year 2021 her dream of becoming a published author came true when she published Loyal Snakes I and Harris I. Since then she has published Misuse Book of Stories, Harris II and Loyal Snakes II all urban fiction.

Publishing books comes last to Rosa's greatest accomplishments of becoming a mother and graduating from college. In all her accomplishments Rosa was determined to sacrifice and beat the odds. While raising four children in the inner city. She wanted to show her loved ones that despite the circumstances you can achieve anything you want just by sacrificing and staying focus.

Rosa plans to venture more into her ability to write different genres but she will always have love for urban fiction.

Urban fiction is relatable to my life experiences and journey! All credit is owed to the inspiration and motivation this genre gave me to read as an adolescent and ultimately to become a published author!

Rosa James